CW00865007

The Adventures of

Mr. Bramble Bones:

The Ghost Hunters

By

M. Deborah Bowden

Illustrated by Korey Woods

The Adventures of Mr. Bramble Bones: The Ghost Hunters
by M. Deborah Bowden

Copyright © 2020. All rights reserved.

Published by Pen It! Publications, LLC in the United States of America
812-371-4128 www.penitpublications.com

ISBN: 978-1-952894-61-9

Illustrated by Korey Woods

Mission Statement

The Bramble Bones series begins at the K-1 reading level and progresses to 3. As the books are separate stories rather than a continuation, they can be read in any order. Reading comprehension / opinion questions and vocabulary are included. Bright pictures hold the reader's attention and aid understanding, as loving characters solve various problems.

Thanks to Thoth for his inspiration,

and Bastet for sending me Grimmy

on which this series is based.

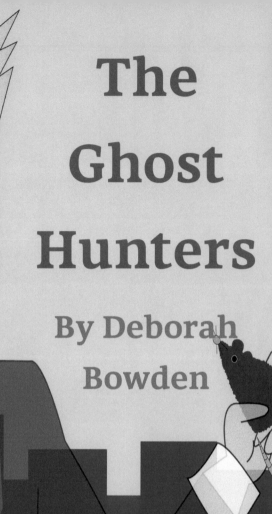

The Ghost Hunters

By Deborah Bowden

Illustrated by Korey Woods

Table of Contents

Chapter 1

Trouble!

Jaxie, the ghost, found a free
wind-up mouse in town.

It had soft fur and tickly whiskers. He wound it up, turned the switch on, and set it down. It squeaked and turned circles. It ran backwards and forwards. It moved very fast.

"Grimmy will like this," he said and he started home.

2

He forgot he couldn't be seen
and the mouse could.
Three teens watched the
mouse run.

Then they watched it float.
They followed and
tried to catch it.

3

Jaxie hid in a bush. The teens gave up, but Jaxie heard them talking.

"A ghost is carrying that mouse," said Tom.

"That ghost must live in the cemetery," said Izzy.

Jeremy said, "Let's go ghost hunting tonight."

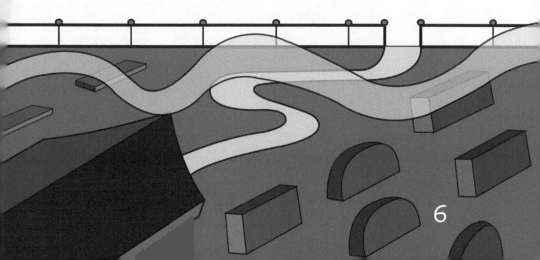

Jaxie raced home while the teens made plans.

7

Chapter 2

Worried!

8

Jaxie was worried. He found Grimmy and Cheeks with Mr. Bramble Bones.

9

He gave Grimmy the
mouse. Then he told
them about the ghost
hunters.

10

"What can we do?"
asked Grimmy.

"Maybe we can scare
them away,"
said Cheeks.

"We don't know how to
be scary," said Jaxie.

11

"Those teens will tell others we live here. Then many ghost hunters will come," said Mr. Bramble Bones.

"We can't have tea parties or play games," said Jaxie. "We'll have to hide all the time."

"I can't go swimming.   Someone might kidnap Grimmy if he goes fishing," said Mr. Bramble Bones.

Grimmy
started crying.

14

Mr. Bramble Bones said, "We must be very quiet tonight. If they can't find ghosts, they'll go away. Tell everyone the plan."

15

Chapter 3

Quiet!

Z
Z
Z
Z
Z
Z
Z
Z
Z
16
Z

The night was dark and quiet.
All the ghosts hid.
Mr. Bramble Bones and Grimmy
stayed home. He had his new
mouse. Cheeks joined them.

"Lock the door, Daddy, please! I'm so scared," cried Grimmy.

"You're safe in here, Grimmy. Just be quiet so those teens won't hear you."

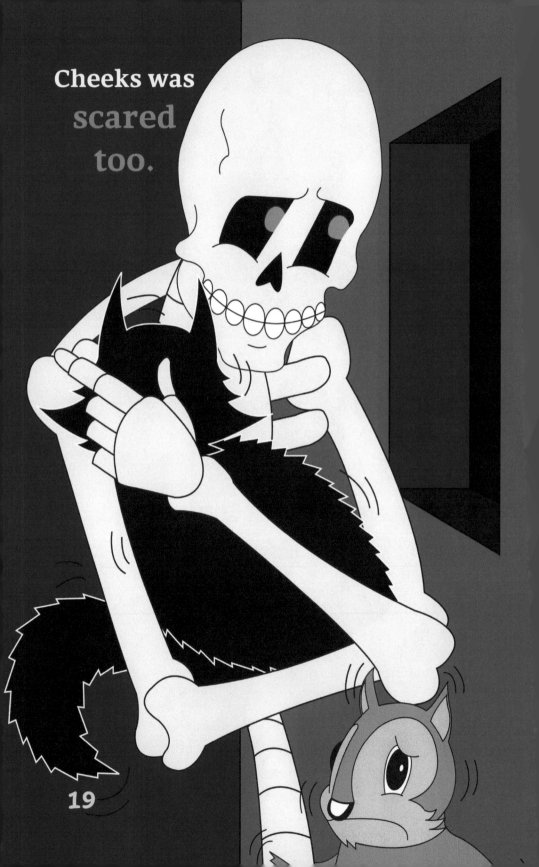

By midnight, Cheeks and Grimmy were bored. "Can we play with the mouse?" they asked. "We promise not to turn it on."

Mr. Bramble Bones lay down for a nap.

"Yes," he said, "but be very quiet. I hear the ghost hunters."

He yawned and fell asleep.

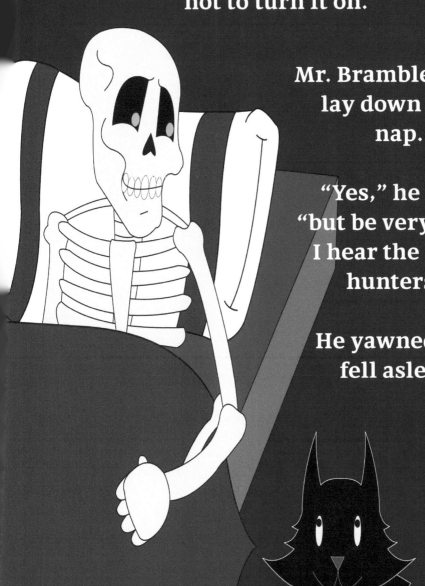

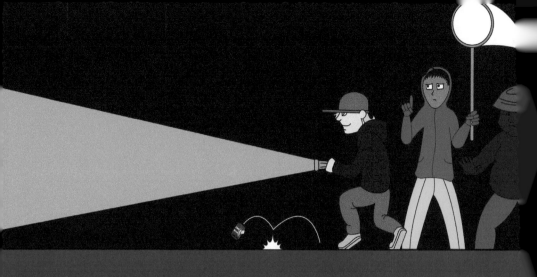

Every ghost could hear
the teens.
They were loud.
They shined their flashlights
on everyone's house.
Then they sat on the ground
and listened.

It was very quiet. Cheeks and Grimmy thought the ghost hunters were gone.

They played keep-away with the mouse. Cheeks jumped onto Mr. Bramble Bones' bed.

He shouted, "Come get the mouse, Grimmy. Catch me."

The teens heard.

They ran to Mr. Bramble Bones' house. They rattled the door. They tried to get in.

Grimmy climbed onto his bed and hit under his blanket.

Cheeks clung to Mr. Bramble Bones.

23

Cheeks had the mouse
and accidentally bumped
the switch.
The mouse turned on.
It squeaked and scared him.

Squeeeek!!! Squeeeek!!!
Squeeeek!!!

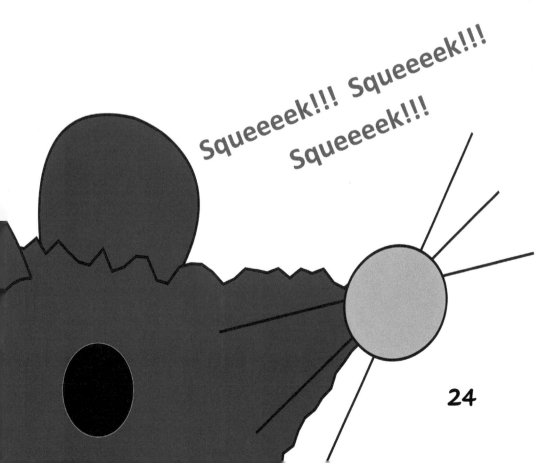

24

Cheeks dropped it
inside Mr. Bramble
Bones' ribs. It ran
around and around.
Its long whiskers
tickled and tickled.

Mr. Bramble
Bones laughed
in his sleep.

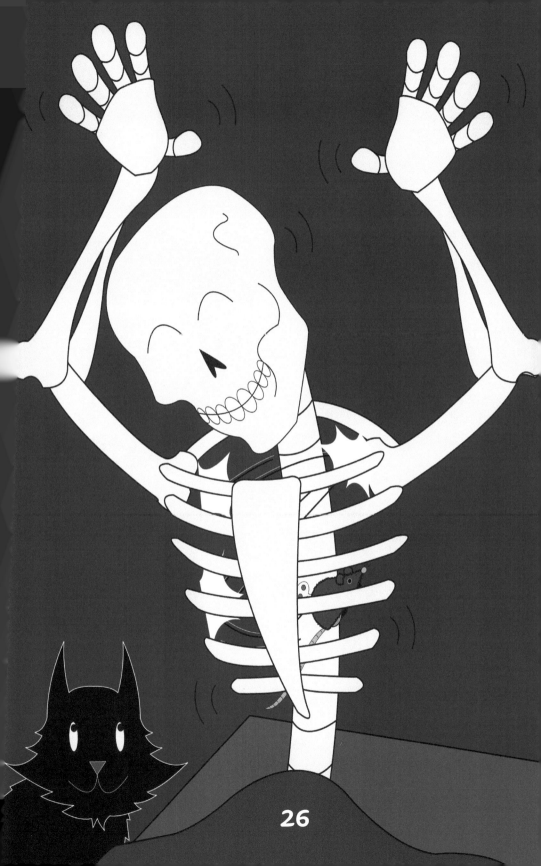

It squeaked again. Mr. Bramble Bones' eyes opened, and he laughed harder.

He tried to grab the mouse, but it was too fast. The more he tried, the more it tickled his ribs. And the more he laughed.

28

"Cheeks, Grimmy, catch it!" he said.

Cheeks tried and missed.

Grimmy caught it with his claws.

"Here, Daddy," he said. He gave Mr. Bramble Bones the mouse.

Squeeeek!!!

29

Mr. Bramble Bones was still laughing.
"Shiver me timbers, boys, I'm going
to get you!"

He grabbed Grimmy and Cheeks
and hugged them.

Izzy yelled,
"Don't tell anyone.
They'll laugh
at us."

Izzy and Tom heard.
They didn't want the ghost to
get them.
They ran away as fast as they
could.

Jeremy stood still
and smiled.

"Grandpa used to
say, 'Shiver me
timbers, boy, I'm
going to get you!'
Then he'd hug me."

Jeremy Bohnes knocked on the door. "I'll be back, Grandpa," he said.

He whistled happily as he walked home.

The End

Reading Comprehension and Opinion
Question and Answers

Ghost Hunters

Below are possible questions which can be used to gauge a child's understanding of the story, if so desired. A few require a child's opinion. Some or all may be asked or others substituted. This is NOT a test.

1. What did Jaxie find in town for Grimmy?
　　Accept: a toy mouse

2. Who saw Jaxie and the mouse?
　　Accept: teens; ghost hunters; Izzy, Tom, and Jeremy.

3. Why were Mr. Bramble Bones, Jaxie, Cheeks, and Grimmy scared?
　　Opinion, possible answers: they'd have to hide all the time, no tea parties or games, no swimming, Grimmy could be kidnapped, more ghost hunters would come.

4. What did Mr. Bramble Bones and all the others plan to do?
　　Accept: everyone be quiet

　　Why? Opinion, possible answers: the ghost hunters would go away, not know ghosts lived there, no more ghost hunters would bother them, could live quietly.

5. Who was Jeremy Bohnes?
　　Accept: Mr. Bramble Bones' grandson.

35

Vocabulary

These words are for older grades.

Do you know what they mean?

accidentally (4th)

clung (4th)

whiskers (4th)

wound (3rd)

cemetery (6th)

switch (4th)

whistled (4th)

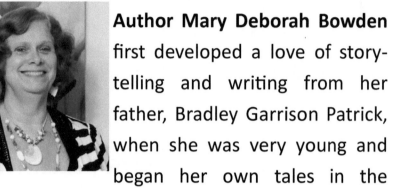**Author Mary Deborah Bowden** first developed a love of story-telling and writing from her father, Bradley Garrison Patrick, when she was very young and began her own tales in the 1970s. She especially enjoys writing about animals for children. She taught English and creative writing in public schools and college for 25 years before retiring to raise her daughter, Erin Bradleigh, on whom she honed her talents.

Originally from Hartford, Kentucky, she moved to Union City, Indiana and then to Greenville, Ohio. There she grew up and graduated. She has been in love with Brown County, Indiana since her Ball State friends enticed her here in early 1970. She knew she had finally found her home.

Other Books by Deborah Bowden

Mr. Bramble Bones and Grimmy Share a Home

Mr. Bramble Bones and Grimmy Clean Up

Mr. Bramble Bones is too Cold to Play

Mr. Bramble Bones and the Mystery of the Missing Blue Blanket

Mr. Bramble Bones: A Christmas to Remember

Felicia Tales: The Many Misadventures of Felicia Brown

The Sack Lunch

Horace the Misunderstood Buzzard

 CPSIA information can be obtained
at www.ICGtesting.com
Printed in the USA
BVHW022341221020
591609BV00021B/10